MARTIAL ARTS IN ACTION

KARATE

MARTIAL ARTS IN ACTION

KARATE

BY TERRY ALLAN HICKS

Marshall Cavendish
Benchmark
New York

This book is dedicated, with deepest respect and gratitude, to the karate instructors and students of Ryokubi Dojo in Stamford, Connecticut.

Published by Marshall Cavendish Benchmark
An imprint of Marshall Cavendish Corporation

Other Marshall Cavendish Offices:
Marshall Cavendish International (Asia) Private Limited, 1 New Industrial Road, Singapore 536196 • Marshall Cavendish International (Thailand) Co Ltd. 253 Asoke, 12th Flr, Sukhumvit 21 Road, Klongtoey Nua, Wattana, Bangkok 10110, Thailand • Marshall Cavendish (Malaysia) Sdn Bhd, Times Subang, Lot 46, Subang Hi-Tech Industrial Park, Batu Tiga, 40000 Shah Alam, Selangor Darul Ehsan, Malaysia

Marshall Cavendish is a trademark of Times Publishing Limited

All websites were available and accurate when this book was sent to press.

Library of Congress Cataloging-in-Publication Data

Hicks, Terry Allan.
Karate / Terry Allan Hicks.
p. cm. — (Martial arts in action)
Includes index.
ISBN 978-0-7614-4934-8
1. Karate—Juvenile literature. I. Title.
GV1114.3.H546 2011
796.815'3—dc22
2010013818

Editor: Peter Mavrikis
Publisher: Michelle Bisson
Art Director: Anahid Hamparian
Series design by Kristen Branch

Photo Research by Candlepants Incorporated

Cover Photo: Radius Images / Alamy Images

The photographs in this book are used by permission and through the courtesy of:
Getty Images: Siri Stafford, 3; Sam Diephuis, 6, 36; Jamie Squire, 13; Absodels, 33; Jamie McDonald, 37; Peter Cade, 38; DK Stock/Eric Glenn, 41; 23. *Alamy Images*: Enigma, 8; Mitch Diamond, 10; Purestock, 11; Sally and Richard Greenhill, 12; Marka, 14; Doug Steley C., 16; Radius Images, 24; ImageState, 28; conceptofstock, 29; Huntstock, Inc, 32. *Corbis*: M.A.Pushpa Kumara/epa, 18; Werner Forman, 20. *Rich Chiu*: 26, 30, 42, 43. *The Image Works*: Syracuse Newspapers/Lassman, 35.
Every effort has been made to locate copyright holders of the images used in this book. If you are a copyright holder or know a copyright holder, please contact us so that we can arrange for appropriate licenses.

Printed in Malaysia (T)
1 3 5 6 4 2

CONTENTS

CHAPTER ONE

THE WAY OF THE EMPTY HAND

IT IS A WINTER EVENING, and a dozen young people are entering an ordinary-looking building in a small city in New England. They come from many different backgrounds. There are both boys and girls, and they range in age from seven to sixteen. They are talking and laughing, but when they take off their coats— and their shoes and socks—their behavior changes completely. They become very serious, because they are here for a very serious reason—to study karate.

Karate is a martial art, a system of fighting **techniques** that came to the Western world from Japan. People who practice karate use **blocks**, **blows**, and kicks, as well as **throwing** and **pinning**

MANY DIFFERENT KINDS OF PEOPLE STUDY KARATE, AND FOR MANY DIFFERENT REASONS.

movements, to protect themselves without weapons. These "empty hand" techniques enable them to defend themselves against larger or stronger attackers. Millions of people around the world practice karate for self-defense, as a competitive sport, or simply for physical exercise.

All the students, known as **karateka**, wear simple white cotton robes, called **gis**, and practice barefoot. The only noticeable difference in their appearance is the color of the heavy cloth belts knotted at their waists. They are green, blue, purple, or brown. The belts show the **kyu**, or skill level, that the karateka have achieved. They are a source of great pride, because they represent months, even years, of hard work.

BY REPEATING THE SAME MOVEMENTS OVER AND OVER AGAIN, THESE KARATE STUDENTS WILL IMPROVE THEIR SELF-DEFENSE SKILLS.

The main area of this karate school, or **dojo**, is a large open space. Before the karateka enter this area, they face it, backs straight, hands at their sides, and bow deeply from the waist. This bow, or *rei*, is a way of displaying respect for the dojo, for its instructors and students, and for the principles of the martial art. The karateka also bow to one another, and they will bow many more times before the evening's class is over.

The dojo is lined with mirrors, so that the karateka can watch their own movements for mistakes. The floor is padded, to protect them against serious injury. Some of the same pieces of exercise equipment found in any Western gym—a punching bag and heavy medicine balls—can be found here. But there are also some unfamiliar sights, such as a padded post, called a *makiwara*, that is used to practice blows. And there are weapons hanging on the walls, including six-foot-long wooden staffs called *bos* and three-pronged metal *sais*. The few decorations include the American and Japanese flags and, in a place of honor, a faded black-and-white photograph of an elderly Asian man. This is Gichin Funakoshi, the person most responsible for bringing karate to the modern world.

This is an intermediate-level class, with students who have already learned many basic karate techniques. From the moment they enter the dojo floor, they begin practicing blows and kicks and the complex, dancelike movements known as **kata**.

Some of the karateka are practicing with special concentration, because they are just a few days away from a promotion test that will determine whether they will move on to the next kyu and the next belt level. After a few minutes of free practice, the karateka

BY WATCHING THEIR MOVEMENTS IN THE MIRROR, KARATEKA CAN CORRECT ANY WEAKNESSES IN THEIR TECHNIQUE.

suddenly come to attention. The dojo's **sempai**, or senior student instructor, has entered. She wears the black belt that marks a highly advanced practitioner of karate. The karateka form a straight line facing her, with the most advanced students to her left. Then Sempai joins the students in facing the portrait of Gichin Funakoshi. They all kneel and bow, their foreheads almost touching the floor, in a show of respect called the *seiza*. Sempai turns to face the class again, and the highest-ranking student turns slightly to bow to her and says, *"Sempai ni re"* ("Bow to sempai.") All the karateka bow again, and then rise to begin the evening's training.

The class begins with warm-up exercises, designed to build up agility, flexibility, balance, **stamina**, and speed. Under Sempai's watchful eye, the karateka work through the exercises, counting off in Japanese: "*Ichi, ni, san, shi, go…*" ("One, two, three, four, five…"). Then they practice basic blocks, blows, and kicks, accompanied by a loud cry, the *kiai* or "spirit shout," which helps to focus the mind and body and increase the power of the movement. These sets of movements, known as *kihon*, are the building blocks for more advanced karate techniques. As the karateka work, Sempai moves among them, pointing out mistakes and telling them how to improve their form, and they respond with "*Hai, Sempai!*" ("Yes, Sempai!").

THESE CHILDREN'S WHITE BELTS INDICATE THAT THEY ARE BEGINNING KARATE STUDENTS.

The students' focus becomes sharper, because a new figure has come onto the floor—the dojo's chief instructor, or **sensei**. Sensei, who wears an old, frayed black belt, has achieved an even higher level of skill than Sempai. He begins to lead the class through more and more advanced techniques. These include the intricate kata, combinations of blocks, blows, kicks, and other movements.

If Sensei is not satisfied with the karateka's focus, discipline, or effort, he may order some of them to do pushups or to kneel and watch silently for the rest of the class. He is especially demanding

KARATEKA ALWAYS WORK TOGETHER.

of the more advanced students, because they are expected to help the others and set a good example for them. This principle—that everyone owes a responsibility to the dojo and to one another, a responsibility that increases with skill and experience—is one of the most important in karate.

The students put on padded gloves and pair off to begin **sparring** practice. They are careful not to hit each other in the face or other sensitive parts of the body, and the padded gloves and flooring help to protect them, but this is serious fighting practice. Still, the

SPARRING PRACTICE ON THE DOJO FLOOR.

karateka always show great respect for one another. A student who is knocked to the floor can always expect his opponent to help him up. And every sparring match ends with a bow.

The class is not all hard work and fighting, however. If the instructors are satisfied with the students' performance, they may lead them in games. The games are designed to help improve the karatekas' skills, but they are also fun. The students may jump on and off balance beams, run an obstacle course, or compete in a tug-of-war.

KARATE STUDENTS SHOW RESPECT, FOR ONE ANOTHER AND FOR THEIR MARTIAL ART, BY BOWING.

When the class comes to an end, the karateka—most of them sweating and out of breath now—once again form a line facing Sensei and kneel. Sensei calls out, "*Mokuso!*" ("meditate") and the karateka close their eyes in a few moments of meditation, focusing their thoughts inward and meditating. Sempai says, "*Sensei ni re.*" The sensei and the students, still kneeling, exchange bows.

Mental discipline is at least as important in karate as physical ability, and this moment of meditation is an essential part of the class. So are the words with which Sensei almost always ends a class. He may tell the karateka to respect their parents, to work hard at their schoolwork, or to follow a healthy diet. Sensei will often tell the students that their karate skills are never to be used outside the dojo, except in self-defense.

The karateka rise, bowing to one another and bowing again to the dojo floor as they leave. The class is over, but most of these students will return at least three times a week. By repeating the techniques they have learned, over and over again, they will improve their fighting skills, and their understanding of the principles of karate.

The students know that karate is far more than simply a set of fighting techniques. It is part of a complete way of life, called karate-do—"the way of the empty hand." This way of life has its roots in Asian traditions and beliefs that are hundreds, even thousands, of years old.

THE HISTORY OF KARATE

CHAPTER TWO

THE MARTIAL ARTS ARE ALMOST AS OLD as recorded history. The word "martial" comes from Mars, the name the ancient Romans gave their god of war. Fighting has always been part of human life, and people have always needed to defend themselves. Martial arts are practiced all over the world, but today, the term usually refers to Asian fighting practices.

The Asian martial arts probably began with contact between the peoples of India and China more than two thousand years ago. India has many ancient martial arts, and some of them certainly influenced the Chinese. The Japanese martial arts, in turn, were deeply influenced by Chinese traditions, but karate did not come

THE PEOPLE OF THE RYUKYU ISLANDS HAVE PRACTICED "EMPTY HAND" FIGHTING FOR CENTURIES.

originally from China or even from Japan. Its beginnings were in Ryukyu, a group of islands that reach from the southern coast of Japan almost to the Chinese mainland. These islands are now a part of Japan, known as the Okinawa Prefecture, but they were once independent, with their own language and culture.

For many years, Ryukyu was troubled by fighting between warring clans (family groups). In 1429, a new king united the islands and banned all weapons in an attempt to stop the violence. But the noblemen and warriors of the island kept practicing a traditional weaponless fighting form called Okinawa T'angor Te ("Okinawa

THIS SCULPTURE SHOWING THE ANCIENT MARTIAL ARTS OF THE INDIAN SUBCONTINENT IS ALMOST TWO THOUSAND YEARS OLD.

hand"), named for the kingdom's main island. Some form of this martial art (sometimes simply called *te*, or "hand") may have existed as early as the seventh century CE, but in later centuries a number of new techniques were introduced by Chinese visitors.

The fighting skills of *te* became very important after 1609, when a Japanese clan, the Satsuma, invaded Ryukyu. They continued the weapons ban, and the Ryukyuans looked for ways to defend themselves against the Satsuma samurai, who wore heavy wooden armor and fought with swords and other weapons. The common people secretly learned to fight with their bare hands and feet, toughening themselves by striking their hands and feet repeatedly against wet sand or wooden posts. (Today's makiwara are modern versions of these posts.) Their hardened hands and feet were extremely effective against the Japanese invaders.

The Japanese could not keep the farmers and fishermen of Ryukyu from owning work tools, and many of them became highly effective weapons. Two pieces of wood linked by a metal chain— used to pound grain—became the deadly **nunchaku**. A metal tool used to haul fish into boats became the handheld weapon known as the *sai*. These and many other tools, from simple wooden staffs to sickles for harvesting grain, formed the basis of the traditional Okinawan practice of fighting with weapons called **kobudo**. Kobudo is not part of the way of the empty hand, but it is often practiced by advanced karateka.

In 1879, Okinawa and the rest of the Ryukyu Islands formally became part of Japan. Weapons were still banned, and the Ryukyuan martial arts were usually practiced in secret. But then an Okinawan

THE HEAVY WOODEN ARMOR WORN BY
JAPANESE SAMURAI.

schoolteacher brought them out into the open, and introduced what we now know as karate to Japan and the world beyond. This was Gichin Funakoshi, now known to karateka simply as Gichin-Sensei.

GICHIN FUNAKOSHI

Funakoshi, who was born in 1868, suffered from poor health as a child, and his family did not expect him to live to reach adulthood. But studying with a *te* master helped to strengthen him, and he became a martial arts master. When the Japanese authorities finally allowed martial arts to be practiced openly, he introduced the fighting styles to his students in Okinawa's public schools. He and other Okinawan masters developed the principles and practices now known as karate, and word of this "new" martial art began to spread beyond Okinawa.

Okinawa had become an important port city, and visiting Japanese military officers often requested demonstrations. In 1922, Funakoshi—already fifty-three years old, an advanced age in those days—was asked to display his skills for an audience that included the visiting Japanese crown prince, Hirohito. His demonstration made such an impression that he was invited to move to the Japanese mainland, where he began teaching karate at several Japanese universities.

That same year, he published his first book about the martial arts, *Karate-Do: My Way of Life*, which helped to make him, and karate, famous throughout Japan. Then, in 1936, Funakoshi opened the first karate dojo on the Japanese mainland, in the capital city of Tokyo. He called it Shotokan, from the Japanese words *shoto* ("waving pines")—the pen name that Funakoshi used when writing poetry—and *kan* ("club").

GICHIN FUNAKOSHI, CREATOR OF THE SHOTOKAN SCHOOL OF KARATE.

Funakoshi did not "invent" karate—which includes elements of several different Okinawan fighting styles— and he was not the only teacher to bring it to Japan. His style, which he also called Shotokan, was the most successful in karate's early years, but it was not the only one. Today, there are at least fifteen major types of karate. They vary somewhat in their approaches and their techniques, but most remain close to the principles that Funakoshi and other early karate masters established.

In the late 1930s, Japan entered World War II, fighting against the United States and other countries. The war took a terrible toll on the Japanese people, and Okinawa was the scene of some of the most brutal fighting. Hundreds of thousands of Okinawans died—and many of the historical records tracing the origins of Okinawan martial arts were destroyed—but these tragic events led to the Okinawan martial arts becoming known to the Western world.

KARATE SPREADS TO THE WORLD

Japan lost the war, and in the years that followed, millions of American soldiers were stationed on Okinawa and the rest of Japan. Many of them began studying the "new" martial art of karate. (Even

THIS PHOTOGRAPH, TAKEN IN THE 1950S, SHOWS A JAPANESE KARATE STUDENT DEFENDING HIMSELF AGAINST AN ATTACK WITH THE WOODEN BO.

KARATE IS AN ANCIENT ART, BUT IT IS ALSO AS MODERN AS THESE TWENTY-FIRST-CENTURY STUDENTS.

before the war, karate had begun to spread to other parts of Asia, especially Korea, where it influenced the martial art of tae kwon do.) Some of these soldiers brought karate back to America. The first true karate dojo in the United States was probably one founded by a Japanese sensei in California in 1955.

In a little more than a century, karate has spread from its origins on Okinawa to become one of the most popular and respected martial arts in the world. Karate is now practiced by an estimated 15 million people in at least 65 countries. It has become a popular form of exercise, an essential means of self-defense, a fighting technique used by police and military organizations, and an important competitive sport practiced in tournaments worldwide. Many karateka hope that the martial art will someday be included in the Olympic Games.

By the time he died, in 1958, Gichin-Sensei—the sickly child who was not expected to live—had reached the very advanced age of eighty-eight. And he had lived to see the way of the empty hand practiced in almost every corner of the world.

CHAPTER THREE

KARATE TECHNIQUES AND TRAINING

KARATE TECHNIQUES ARE THE RESULT OF many years of careful study of anatomy—how the human body is made and how it moves—and energy. The early martial arts masters learned to focus a blow or kick for maximum effect, where to strike an opponent's body to cause the greatest impact, and even how to use an attacker's own energy against him.

The martial arts have evolved greatly, but today's karateka use the same basic principles that were used centuries ago. One of the most important principles is to concentrate the greatest possible energy in a comparatively small area. This may mean striking a blow with only the fingertips, or the side of a tightly closed hand, increasing the force of the blow and the impact on the opponent.

THE KARATE STUDENT NEVER STOPS STUDYING AND PRACTICING THE TECHNIQUES OF THE MARTIAL ART.

A VIVID DEMONSTRATION OF THE POWER OF CAREFULLY FOCUSED ENERGY.

Another important principle is that the entire body is used as a weapon, and as much of the body's energy as possible is used. The karateka may do this by turning or shifting the body's weight during a blow or kick. The force of the movement becomes part of the blow, increasing its speed and impact. Taking a deep breath before striking, and letting it out during the blow, also increases its power.

It is also important not to slow down a blow before impact. The karateka aims somewhere beyond the point of impact, so that the blow is still increasing in force when it reaches its target. This is what makes it possible for experienced karateka to break thick wooden boards, bricks, or even heavy pieces of concrete with their bare hands or feet.

STANCES

The **stance**, or *dachi*, is literally the foundation of karate. The different stances give the karateka a low **center of gravity**, making it possible to deliver effective blocks, blows, and kicks, and making it harder to be knocked off balance. There are many

A SOLID STANCE IS ESSENTIAL IN THE MARTIAL ARTS.

different stances, for different body types, different fighting styles, and different types of attacks. The horse stance (*kiba-dachi*), for example, places the karateka with both knees bent and feet parallel to each other— like someone riding a horse—a strong position for dealing with an opponent who is very close. Other stances are better for defending against a taller opponent, or one who is farther away, or, like the attention stance (*musubi-dachi*), simply for showing that the karateka is ready for whatever comes next.

BLOCKS

One of the first lessons every karate student learns is "There is no first blow in karate." Karate skills are meant only for self-defense. This is why every kata begins with a block—a sweeping arm or leg

A KARATEKA USES A MIDDLE BLOCK TO DEFEND HIMSELF AGAINST A REVERSE PUNCH.

movement designed to keep an opponent from landing a blow. The different blocks defend against different types of attacks. The high block (*jodan-uke*), for example, protects against an attack on the upper body and head with fists held tight and arms crossed in front of the chest. A downward block (*gedan barai*) sweeps one arm down to protect against a blow to the lower body. And a knife-hand block (*shuto-uke*) protects against an attack on the midsection, with the fingers of one hand held tightly together in a blade shape, the outside edge facing the attacker.

BLOWS

Blows made with the hand or arm are among the most effective karate techniques. A blow may be a punch, made with a tightly closed fist, or a strike with the fingertips or the inside or outside edge of the hand. The karateka usually "chambers" one arm, holding it tightly against the waist or the side of the head with the fist clenched tight. The chambered fist then strikes out at the opponent, while the other arm moves back to chamber. The force of the blow, whether aimed high or low, comes from the karateka's midsection. This gives it more power, and so does the shifting of the body from the chambering movement.

One of the most basic blows is the straight punch (*oi-zuki*), used to make a powerful impact over a long distance. It begins in a stance with one foot forward, and the karateka delivers a straight blow with the fist on the same side of the body at the forward foot. The reverse punch (*gyaku-zuki*) works the opposite way, using the hand on the same side as the back leg in the karateka's stance.

KICKS

The legs and feet are perhaps the karateka's most powerful weapons, and are often used to deliver a blow from a distance. One basic kick is the front kick (*mae-geri*). The karateka lifts the front leg up, raising the knee high, and places most body weight on the back leg. The front leg kicks out as far as it will go, so that it is almost straight at the point of impact, then is quickly retracted and set back on the floor. In the roundhouse kick (*mawashi-geri*), the body's weight is once again placed on the back leg. But this time, when the front

A YOUNG KARATEKA UNLEASHES THE POWER OF A ROUNDHOUSE KICK.

leg comes up, the knee—bent at a sharp angle in the leg—is almost parallel to the waist. The karateka kicks out, striking with the instep of the foot, then retracts the leg.

Karate also uses movements to immobilize an attacker. They include sweeps, to move the legs out from under an opponent, throws that push or pull the opponent to the floor, and takedowns—grips that force the opponent down. Many of these techniques are designed to use the opponent's momentum against him or her.

KATA

Once the karate student has begun to learn these basic movements, they are combined into the sets of movements called *kata*. Karateka practice the many kata over and over again, improving their form, speed, and balance. Another important goal of kata study is mental discipline. Gichin Funakoshi himself is said to have practiced a single kata for four years before he believed he had mastered it.

The kata, which are practiced both individually and by groups of karateka moving simultaneously, simulate the defenses that the karateka would use to defend against as many as five attackers. Some kata are incredibly complex, with dozens of separate movements that the karateka must perform almost without thinking. And the karateka may ultimately have to master as many as one hundred kata.

THIS "TIME LAPSE" PHOTOGRAPH SHOWS THE SPEED AND POWER OF A TRAINED MARTIAL ARTIST.

One kata is called Heian shodan—the first in the Heian, or "Peace," series of kata. Heian shodan has twenty-two separate components. The karateka begins by bowing, stating the name of the kata, and assuming the ready stance (*yoi-dachi*). Then comes a step and downward block on the left side, followed by a forward-stepping punch with the right fist. Next comes a 180-degree turn, followed by a hammer-fist strike. The movements continue, following each other rapidly, as the karateka defends against imaginary attacks from all sides, turning, blocking, and striking blows. At the end, the karateka returns to the ready stance and bows again.

To a casual observer, these movements are almost impossible to understand, or even follow. But each element of the kata has a specific purpose. And hundreds, even thousands, of repetitions will make it almost second nature—and prepare the karateka for almost any possible type of attack.

KARATE TRAINING

Karate and other martial arts cannot be learned by reading books or watching films or television. These sources — if they are serious and well-informed — can help people decide whether the martial arts are right for them. But films and television often give people a dangerously misleading impression of the martial arts. Children who try to imitate what they see in them will not learn true martial arts skills, and may even hurt themselves. This is why the only way to learn karate is to study at a dojo, with a master of the martial art, a process that takes many years.

YOUNG AND OLD CAN PRACTICE KARATE FOR SELF-DEFENSE, FOR EXERCISE—AND FOR FUN.

Almost anyone can practice karate. Children can begin to study the martial art as early as three years of age, and adults have begun in their fifties and sixties. A new student does not have to be in perfect physical condition or be what is sometimes called a natural athlete. In fact, karate can be extremely helpful to people with severe physical and mental disabilities. Other martial arts schools have students who have had legs or arms amputated and are sometimes in wheelchairs, and one dojo in New York City teaches karate to students who are visually impaired—some of them completely blind. For these students, as for every karateka, what matters most is a serious commitment to studying karate.

Belts and Promotion Testing

Gichin Funakoshi introduced the belt system to karate in the 1920s, adapting the system that was being used in judo. In the beginning, karateka wore only two colors of belt, white and black, and this is still the practice in many Japanese dojos. But most dojos and karate associations now use a more complex system of colors to indicate skill levels, typically ranging from light to dark. Different schools of karate and even different dojos use different belt systems to mark the karateka's advancement. Most, however, begin with white for the new student, and the belts become darker as the student's skill improves. Some of the colors used, in order of advancement, are white, yellow, orange, green, blue, purple, brown, red, and finally black. A stripe is sometimes added to a belt to indicate advancement within that level. And the black-belt level itself has several different levels, called dan, or degrees, within it. These may go as high as tenth dan, an honor that is usually given to only one person at a time— the leader of a particular karate organization.

MANY DIFFERENT ASIAN MARTIAL ARTS USE COLORED BELTS TO MARK A STUDENT'S ACHIEVEMENT.

TOURNAMENT COMPETITION TESTS—AND IMPROVES —KARATEKAS' SKILLS.

TOURNAMENTS AND COMPETITION

Many karateka enjoy competing in tournaments and other sporting events, as a way of testing their skills against opponents from other dojos. Tournaments may simply be meetings between two or more dojos, or much more elaborate competitions run by national or international karate organizations.

Karateka of all ages are judged on the form of their kata, and in sparring competitions where they must fight while remaining in a very restricted area. If they step out of the boundaries of that area, they have lost the competition. Many consider competition one of the high points of karate studies. One of the benefits of competing is that it helps the karateka to sharpen the mental and physical skills that they might need if they are ever really attacked. However, not all karate students are interested in competing, and karateka are not required to do so.

CHAPTER FOUR
KARATE IN EVERYDAY LIFE

PEOPLE STUDY AND PRACTICE KARATE for many different reasons. Some people want to learn skills that can help them defend themselves if they are ever attacked. Many children, for example, take up karate because they are looking for the self-confidence to deal with bullies they may meet in the hallways of their schools or the streets of their neighborhoods. Other karateka approach karate as a competitive sport, and are interested in participating in tournaments and other competitions. Some are simply looking for an interesting and challenging physical activity.

Most karateka will never use the skills they learn in the dojo in self-defense. Most will never be seriously threatened, and most will

MARTIAL ARTS TRAINING IS AN EXCELLENT WAY TO BUILD SELF-CONFIDENCE.

The Dojo KUN

A karate dojo has a set of important rules, first laid down by Gichin Funakoshi, called the dojo kun. All of these rules concern character and behavior, not physical skill. This is one common version of the dojo kun. The word "first" at the beginning of each rule is meant to show that all are equally important.

First, seek perfection of character.
First, protect the truth.
First, foster the spirit of effort.
First, respect the rules of etiquette.
First, guard against impetuous courage.

have the strength, self-discipline, and personal courage to walk away—for example, from a bully—when that is the right thing to do. But a karateka who is attacked and has no choice but to defend himself will be able to do so.

The skills of karate can prove to be useful in unexpected ways. One young karateka learned that when he was suddenly attacked by a dog while walking down the street. He reflexively blocked the dog's bite with a hammer-fist blow that protected him. He was bitten, but was not hurt nearly as badly as if he had not protected himself.

The lessons learned in the dojo extend far beyond fighting and self-defense. A sensei instills the values of "the way of the empty hand"

THE STUDY OF KARATE BUILDS STRENGTH IN BOTH BODY AND MIND.

in every karateka. The focus, discipline, and concentration help karate students in school, at home, and in almost every other aspect of their daily lives. Some claim that karate improves their

KARATE IS HARD WORK—AND A LOT OF FUN.

concentration. This is why the most important lessons learned in a karate dojo are not about fighting, or about athletics, but about the philosophy of karate-do.

All serious karateka are seeking perfection of character in every aspect of their lives. This does not mean that anyone has to be perfect, or even that anyone can ever expect to be perfect. Instead, it means that the karateka goes through his or her entire life—inside and outside the dojo—showing respect for others and trying to live a good, helpful, and useful life.

The principles of the dojo kun have their roots deep in traditions that are thousands of years old. They have been passed on by martial arts masters—some famous, some forgotten—from China, from Okinawa, from Japan, and from many other parts of the world. These values are every bit as meaningful today as they were in the kingdom of Ryukyu hundreds of years ago. And the dedication of the millions of karateka around the world ensures that they will remain meaningful for many years to come.

A KARATE CLASS ENDS AS IT BEGAN—WITH A DISPLAY OF RESPECT.

GLOSSARY

block—A defensive movement that protects against an attack.

blow—A striking movement with the hand or arm.

center of gravity—The point where a person's weight is focused.

dan—A degree of achievement by a karateka who has already earned a black belt.

dojo—A karate school.

gi—A simple white robe (also called a *dojogi*) worn by people who practice karate or some other Japanese martial arts.

karateka—Someone who studies or practices karate.

kata—A complex set of movements that simulates a defense against an imaginary opponent or group of opponents.

kobudo—A traditional Okinawan style of fighting using simple weapons adapted from ordinary tools.

kyu—The level of skill a karateka has achieved, as measured by promotion tests and dedication.

nunchaku—An Okinawan weapon, originally a farmer's tool, made from two blocks of wood linked by a short piece of metal chain.

pinning—Holding an opponent in place so that he or she cannot move.

sempai—The senior student instructor of a dojo (second in authority to the sensei).

sensei—A highly skilled karateka who is the chief instructor at a dojo.

sparring—Fighting practice.

stamina—Physical strength and endurance.

stance—The way you stand and position your body during martial arts movements.

technique—A method or specific way of doing something.

throwing—Pushing or pulling an opponent.

FIND OUT MORE

BOOKS

Cook, Harry. *Karate*. Chicago: Raintree Publishers, 2004.

Crudelli, Chris. *The Way of the Warrior: Martial Arts and Fighting Styles from Around the World*. London: Dorling Kindersley, 2008.

Olhoff, Jim. *Martial Arts Around the Globe*. Minneapolis, MN: ABDO & Daughters, 2008.

Reilly, Robin L. *Karate for Kids*. North Clarendon, VT: Tuttle Publishing, 2004.

WEBSITES

Amateur Athletic Union of the USA
http://aaukarate.org

Interntional Shotokan Karate Federation
http://www.iskf.com

kidsaskSensei
http://www.asksensei.com/kids.htm

INDEX

ABOUT THE AUTHOR

Terry Allan Hicks has written more than twenty titles for Marshall Cavendish Benchmark Books, on subjects as diverse as the common cold and the planet Saturn. He lives in Connecticut with his wife, Nancy, and their three sons, James—a very serious student of karate—Jack, and Andrew.